Dr. Judittle

Also by Judean W. Etheredge

Cabin by the Lake
Cabin in the Pines
Cabin by the Bridge

Dr. Judittle

A book about animals by
Judean W. Etheredge

iUniverse, Inc.
New York   Bloomington

Dr. Judittle

Unless otherwise noted, all Scriptures are taken from the King James Version of the Bible.

iUniverse books may be ordered through booksellers or by contacting:

iUniverse
1663 Liberty Drive
Bloomington, IN 47403
www.iuniverse.com
1-800-Authors (1-800-288-4677)

ISBN: 978-1-4401-8416-1 (sc)
ISBN: 978-1-4401-8417-8 (ebk)

Printed in the United States of America

iUniverse rev. date: 10/20/2009

For

Richard Shane Etheredge
And
All Animal Lovers

"The wolf also shall dwell with the lamb, and the leopard shall lie down with the kid; and the calf and the young lion and the fatling together; and a little child shall lead them."

Isaiah 11:6

Contents

Prologue

As I stand gazing over the leaf covered markers, I remember so many little friends. Pet Cemetery began in 1988 when I moved the remains of my little friend Eleanor from her previous place of internment to her new waiting ground. Over the past twenty-one years, the cemetery has almost reached full capacity. My husband and I have already made plans for an extension.

Simple little markers of concrete with names scratched to preserve their memory rise above the ground. Many tears filled the holes as each animal was laid to rest. It is not their deaths on which I want to dwell; it is their lives.

Not all the animals end up in Pet Cemetery. Dozens of animals including opossums, rabbits, squirrels, birds, chipmunks, foxes, snakes, and turtles have been released. Some have just visited on their way to other places.

The saddest cases are those who simply disappear. I have searched for weeks for cats that should not have left home. Fearing they may have been injured in the highway, I have walked the roadsides in vain looking for them.

Ever since I was little, I played doctor and tried to help as many animals as I could. Because of my youth and inexperience, many little lives were lost; however, there were some that survived. These survivors gave me the motivation to continue. It was because of the movie *Dr. Dolittle* that I acquired the name Dr. Judittle.

We are blessed now with the Internet which answers just about any question one may have about the care of an animal. That is, if one has the time to research. Before the Internet and before the laws that regulated the care of wild animals, one had to do the best with the knowledge one had.

I would like to share a few of the stories of some of the animals that came in and out my life in hopes that you can laugh with me in my ignorance, cry with me in the loss of my friends, and strive with me to make this world a better place for animals whose only voice is you.

Chapter 1
Ms. Walley

Can you imagine going to your car in the Wal-mart parking lot late one night to find a woman crawling around under it and a man standing beside it holding a purse? My husband and I found ourselves in such a situation. Let me explain.

It was our usual night to visit Wal-mart where my husband and I buy bulk quantities of cat food, dog food, old nuts and various other foods consumed by our eighty animals. As we started to the car, I glanced to my right just in time to see a car narrowly miss hitting a small kitten which appeared to be trying to make its way to the other side of the street to come to me. Okay, maybe I imagined the part about the kitten coming to me, but I did see the car almost hit the kitten.

I looked at my husband and said, "Ohooo!" I think it was at that point he realized we would be adding another cat to our already large family of critters.

I scurried across the parking lot to retrieve the kitten, but it ran under a car. So down on my all fours I went calling for the kitten. Calling is a little "meow" sound I make that sometimes sounds like another cat. This little kitten didn't respond to my call. As I crawled toward it, it somehow managed to always stay just three inches from my reach. It was at this point I asked my husband to hold my purse so I could maneuver myself further under the car. I was in this position, half under the car and half out, when the owner approached. I explained what I was doing under her car and she smiled politely at me and left. By this time, the kitten had moved over to the next car. My husband, who is a patient man I might add, was beginning to feel a bit impatient. I don't know if he was imagining me crawling all over the parking lot or that he just felt ridiculous standing there holding my purse. Anyway, he wanted this situation to resolve itself, quickly.

Then a miracle occurred. I found a chicken bone lying right under the car in front of my own nose. Now I had something the kitten wanted. I could negotiate.

As you might expect, the owner of the second car appeared and my husband was doing his best to explain to her why he was holding a purse and why his wife was under her car holding a chicken bone. By that time, the chicken bone had worked its magic and I had the kitten in hand. At this point, the kitten was supposed to bite and scratch me but she didn't. She settled into my arms and as quick as a flash my husband had our car cranked and we were on our way home.

The kitten was introduced to our other nine cats and she made herself at home. She won our hearts and became our inside cat. We named her Ms. Walley after the Wal-mart store.

Once I was called to rescue a kitten that had fallen from the attic of a house to the floor inside the wall joist. There was no way to reach the kitten except to tear the shower wall out. With the permission of the owner, this was done. It was a two week old kitten that had stayed inside the wall "meowing" for three days. I took it home not knowing if it would live or die. It was touch and go for awhile but the kitten finally came around.

Ms. Walley, now grown, was intrigued with the kitten. When I first introduced the two, Ms. Walley thought that was the dirtiest kitten she had ever seen. The reason I know this is because she gave that kitten a licking from the tip of its nose to the tip of its tail.

One night, I put Ms. Walley outside. Shortly afterwards I heard a muffled *meow* at the back door. I flipped the light on to see Ms. Walley with a very large rat in her mouth. With her meow, she was letting me know she wanted back inside. She wanted to bring the big rat inside with her to feed the kitten. I tried to explain to her that we didn't bring large, ugly rats into the house dead or alive. But for her sake I did take the kitten outside and let her smell the rat. I thanked Ms. Walley for her thoughtfulness. I knew Ms. Walley would be a good mother to the kitten. And she was. She taught it to hunt and to play and to defend itself and many more maternal things that we will never fully understand. I think she slipped a lesson in there that "cats rule" because that little kitten developed *some* kind of attitude.

Ms. Walley won our hearts in more ways. She would slip into bed with us and wake us up in the middle of the night wanting to play. She could play chess like no other cat I've seen. With one swoop of her tail, she could move three pawns, one knight and maybe a rook or two. Her favorite game was running from one end of the house to the other. I think she was timing herself because each time she did it, it became faster. She loved the comfort of a lap and when she caught me reading would make herself comfortable in my lap. The next thing I knew I was peeping over her fuzzy little body trying to focus on my book.

She won our hearts for almost four years. One afternoon she slipped into my lap and lay there so quietly. I remember putting her on the floor so I could take my bath. My husband noticed her breathing heavily and we just thought maybe she had eaten something that didn't agree with her. She had been outside most of the afternoon. We went about our business but kept an eye on her. About 2:00 in the early morning I was awakened by her loud "meows." As my husband and I approached her, we could tell that she was in much distress. In a few moments, she was dead. She had died a painful death. In the dark hours of the night, we laid her to rest in Pet Cemetery. As with each animal that we grow to love and lose, we buried a piece of our hearts with her.

Chapter 2
Queen Solomene

To understand how Queen Solomene came to stay with us for a few weeks, one would have to understand the nature of my mother. The best way to describe her was that she was *phobic*. My mama was afraid of lizards, green frogs, snakes or just about any little creature that could hop, fly or crawl.

I was walking around Mama's house one afternoon enjoying her beautiful flowers when I kept finding what appeared to be little frog skeletons. They were everywhere.

"Mama," I asked, "why are there so many dead frogs around your house?"

"I've been killing them with hot water," she said without remorse.

"But why?" I asked.

"You know if one of those little creatures hopped on me, I would simply die. At night they stick to my screens.

I boil a pot of water and when it gets good and hot, I dash it on them."

No need to say anything else. She had found a way to kill green frogs not realizing that she was upsetting the eco system which kept her flowers so beautiful.

One Saturday morning I was busy in my office when I received a telephone call from Mama. As I picked up the telephone, Mama was already talking.

"It almost killed me!" echoed through the receiver.

"What did, Mama?" I asked.

"That snake," she screamed. "It chased me all over the yard. Do you want it?"

"What kind of snake is it?"

"It's a chicken snake. I called your brother to come kill it for me but he wouldn't and wants to know if you want it."

"Okay, Mama, I'll take it if he brings it to me."

While waiting on my brother to bring me a chicken snake, I cleaned out an aquarium I hadn't used in years. All the time I'm thinking, *is there such a snake as a chicken snake?* Mama had a way of naming things. If she saw a snake near a chicken, it was a chicken snake. If she saw one close to a lizard, it was a lizard snake.

I layered the bottom of the aquarium with rocks and wood to give it an indigenous look. Then I placed a bowl of water inside and was wondering what food a chicken snake would eat. *Eggs, of course.* So I placed an egg inside the aquarium and called myself ready for the little snake when my brother brought it over.

When my brother arrived, I showed him my proud habitat inside the 20 gallon aquarium. He stared at the aquarium and cocked his head to one side. When he cocked his head, I knew I was in trouble.

"I guess it will fit in there," he said.

He then dumped the box he was holding upside down and immediately the inside of the aquarium became a blur, a mixture of flying pebbles and angry snake trying to get out.

After I pried my fingernails from the porch railing where I had taken refuge, I said, "This is not a chicken snake. This is a King snake and it's the biggest one I've ever seen.

"It's a King snake, alright. Glad you took him. I didn't want to kill the little fellow. I'll be on my way." And with that my brother was gone.

We have always cherished King snakes around the farm. They are one of the few snakes that actually kill poisonous snakes. The poisonous venom of the rattle snakes and the moccasins which live around us, do not harm the King snakes.

I wasn't disappointed that it was a King snake. I preferred having it rather than a chicken snake, although I had not expected it to be so large. The problem I now faced was the egg I had placed inside the aquarium. The egg had to be removed before this thirty-six inch long King Snake rolled over on it and crushed it. I didn't relish the idea of sticking my hand into the aquarium to retrieve it.

I've always had this system that as soon as my husband came in from work, I would immediately tell him all the bad things that had happened that day or all the things I had torn up that day. That way he would have longer to work on the problems and fix them. My husband removed the egg from the aquarium.

I caught a chameleon and placed it in the aquarium to see if the snake had a taste for something green. The next morning it was gone. I felt bad for the chameleon but went straight out and caught another one and placed it in the aquarium for the snake's next meal.

During the next week, I observed snake behavior. One morning after a long nap, the snake began to stir and opened its mouth and yawned. How often does one get to see a snake yawn? I found this quite fascinating. Often the snake would crawl over the pebbles and approach the lizard and stick its tongue out and crawl off. I learned later that the tongue served as a sense of smell. Once the snake crawled into the water bowl and spun around several times. Was he swimming or just taking a bath? I had to just wonder on that one.

Because the Scriptures tell us to be "wise as serpents" (Matthew 10:16) and King Solomon was the wisest king who ever lived, I name the snake King Solomon.

I placed the aquarium in my office which I kept open during the week days. On Saturdays and Sundays, I would check on King Solomon just to make sure he had not crawled out of the aquarium.

One Sunday morning as I approached the aquarium, I noticed something different. King Solomon was lying on a pile of white rocks. But I knew I hadn't placed any white rocks in the aquarium. I discovered they were not rocks, but eggs. King Solomon was laying eggs. I stood in awe as I watched the snake's body constrict and then relax. Another egg was coming. It was then that King Solomon gave me the greatest gift, seeing her lay her thirteenth and final egg. I renamed her Queen Solomene after that morning.

How often do we take nature for granted not seeking to understand nor interact with it? When God created the living creatures, the cattle, the creeping things, the beast of the earth, He looked upon it and saw that it was good (Gen. 1:24-25). God gave man the responsibility to have dominion over every living thing that moveth upon the earth. Man was given the duty of caregiver.

Queen Solomene had shared something special with me. She had allowed me to observe her naps, her yawns, her baths and the start of her family. It was time for her liberation. I took her to a secret place and allowed her to crawl away. She paused for a moment as if to look up at me and say goodbye, then crawled away into the woods.

Chapter 3
Phene, Nome, and Non

I define a *dilemma* as a predicament you get yourself into when you don't know exactly what to do to fix it, like the one I am about to tell you.

One Friday afternoon, I looked out my kitchen window and saw my sister-in-law approaching the house with a shoebox under her arm. Something told me she wasn't bringing me a pair of shoes. Sure enough, she had for me three baby squirrels. Their nest in the top of a pine tree had been destroyed by timber cutters and without proper nurturing, these little babies would die. They were very small and would need feeding every two to three hours with a pet nurser, a tiny bottle like the one used for baby kittens.

Looking at baby squirrels requires imagination. It's kind of like what Michelangelo felt as he looked at large blocks of uncut marble. He would often go to the quarry himself and select these large chunks of stone. He said he could see the sculpture inside just waiting to get out. Baby squirrels are like that. When you look at those little pink, hairless, finger-like objects with knots where the eye sockets are suppose to be, you really have to see the cute little furry squirrel it was meant to be. Then there are the large, bony, oversized hands and that tail, that hideous, rat-like tail that you have to endure as you devote your time to nurturing these little animals. Well, I accepted these little babies and assumed the responsibility of nurturing them because I really didn't know how to say *no*.

This is where the dilemma came in. My husband had just received his first day off after working twelve to sixteen hours per day for the past four months at a new job. He was ready to go somewhere. There I was, stuck with a box full of hairless creatures that needed feeding every two to three hours at least for the first week. I could have told him, "Well, dear we really can't go anywhere on your day off because I have to stay home and feed three little baby squirrels." I was much smarter than that. I replied, "I'm ready when you are."

The next morning I packed formula (diluted can milk), a thermos full of hot water and a purse lined with soft cloth. I placed the baby squirrels in the bottom of the purse. I kept the purse in my lap for the next ninety-three miles as we drove to the City. Country folks have to drive long distances to find a fancy place to eat out and maybe catch a movie. My body heat kept the babies warm which is important for their survival. On route, when the babies needed feeding, I poured their formula into their bottle and placed it in a cup of hot water from the thermos to warm it a bit. At the appropriate temperature, I fed each little baby and placed it back into its nest in the bottom of my purse. This went on every two to three hours all day long.

The purse went with me into our favorite eating establishment. The waitresses were unaware of the contents of my purse. I was sipping the last swallows of my coffee with the purse snug in my lap when I looked over at an elderly lady stuffing chocolate chip cookies from the dessert bar into her purse. I envisioned then a check point at the exit door and all the waitresses checking the pockets and purses of everyone leaving trying to find the missing chocolate chip cookies. I visualized the elderly lady slipping on by with her sweet smile and me standing holding the purse not wanting anyone to look inside. "Guilty!" the waitresses would scream as they tried to drag me off to jail with the purse safe in my clutches. Then it would happen. The purse would be pried from my tightly clasped fingers and opened. Upon looking at the contents, the waitresses would scream and run and then I would be standing. . .

"Judy, if you're finished, let's go," my husband said bringing me out of my hypothetical scenario.

The purse went with me to our favorite bookstore as I browsed the aisles looking for books on squirrels. The purse went with me to our favorite building supply store as my husband bought many items on his list. Then we visited the mall.

I was being very careful how I carried the purse so as not to squash the babies and was unaware that I was holding the purse high and close to me. My husband said, "Don't hold the purse like that. Someone is going to think you have a bomb." I tried from then on not to call attention to myself.

Phenomenon was playing at the cinema in the mall. I watched the movie with my purse on my lap. I had fed the squirrels outside in the car before entering the cinema. Little squirrels like to squirm and as I sat there watching the movie and eating my popcorn, I could feel the movements of three contented babies. I named the squirrels Phene, Nome and Non after the movie.

The squirrels grew into healthy adults. Their tails gradually fuzzed out and their big bright eyes opened. I kept them inside until they were old enough to be placed in the habitat. In the habitat their instincts took over as they learned to bury nuts and climb trees but most of all to become less dependent upon me. This was their transition period from living with people to learning to live in the wild.

I guess the best times with them were the times I sat with them in the habitat. The habitat is equipped with a hollow log, a pool, several nesting baskets, hanging limbs and all they care to eat. I remember many afternoons I sat on the hollow log as the growing babies climbed all over me burying pecans, peanuts and acorns in my pockets and hair. They loved to jump from tree to hair and from hair to tree. Just like children they had to learn how to leave a safe environment and learn to live in a wild and wicked world.

To help the squirrels make the adjustment from their safe habitat to the wild, I had to distance myself from them. During this period, I would only place food in the habitat. I gradually weaned myself from having any other contact with them.

As I observed three adult squirrels one day, running and climbing all over the habitat, I knew they were ready to be released. Still, I wanted to be able to identify them for a little while after they were released. They were much too wild to hold now, so a tag of any sort was out of the question. I gave it a lot of thought and it just came to me, the perfect solution. I would spray them with a color which would last maybe a week or two. Food coloring would be the perfect coloring. Only, I needed a way to spray it onto the squirrels. I searched in my art supplies for an atomizer but could not locate one. I would just use drinking straws.

I set my homemade *squirrel identification kit* up outside the habitat. I had three plastic cups with a straw in each one. I then poured enough food coloring in each to be able to suck up with a straw. I decided to use the red, blue and the green colors.

I sucked a straw full of red coloring and pointed the straw toward the habitat. A squirrel ran by at lightning speed. I blew on the straw and red coloring sprayed out into the air hitting nothing. I repeated the process. I sprayed blue coloring, again missing the fast moving squirrel. Now, I had only one color left, the green. I sucked too hard on the straw and ended up with a mouth full of green coloring. I looked at my hands which were multicolored. My clothes were speckled with red, blue and green.

My little brainstorm had turned into a disaster. I'd wasted my entire box of food coloring. I'd colored myself rather than the squirrels. As I was standing in the habitat lamenting my predicament, my husband came in from work. I realized then that I'd just added a new dimension to the word *dilemma.*

Chapter 4
Digger, Swimmer, Barker...
and then came Jennie

It was a very cold morning, in the low twenties, as I recall. Believe me, here in the South, that is cold. My husband had just left for work and I was gazing out the window as I washed the morning dishes. My mind was out of gear waiting for the caffeine from the morning coffee to kick in. I was brought back to reality when I saw my husband walking back up the driveway. My heart sank as I watched him. I had seen him do this so many times before, bring one of our cats that had been killed by the morning traffic. This time he did not head toward the pet cemetery but walked toward the house. He was carrying something in his arms. By this time, I had met him at the door. He gently handed me three small puppies someone had just dumped off at the end of our driveway. Had my husband not found them, they would have frozen.

They were such adorable little puppies that one hardly noticed the sores, patches of missing fur, and pustules spread over their little bodies. They had sarcoptic mange. I promptly took them to the vet for treatment for mange, worming, and immunizations. After several months of dips and lots of TLC, the puppies became healthy, energetic little dogs.

Although they were of mixed breed, I called them my little lab puppies. They named themselves. Swimmer, who is our lab with greyhound-like features, was so named because she could not stay out of the pond. I embarrassed myself one morning. I was watching her swim and after an hour in the pond she showed no signs of coming out. I thought something was terribly wrong with her. Like maybe she had exhausted herself swimming and didn't have the strength to make it out of the water. She would swim to the edge but would turn and go back into the deep. As quickly as I could, I pushed the canoe into the water for the rescue. I paddled furiously to try and catch her but she kept herself at arms length from the canoe. I soon became exhausted and desperate not knowing how to rescue my poor little drowning puppy. Then without giving me a second glance, she swam to the bank, ran out, shook the water off, and engaged in playful running with her siblings. I sat in the canoe, exhausted from the ordeal and feeling rather silly. The dog just loved the water.

Barker, our lab with beagle-like features, started barking at an early age. Usually, you don't have to worry about puppies barking when they have playmates. They may engage in frisky growls especially when pulling on something like a towel drying on the clothesline or when ripping your husband's uniforms to shreds that were laid out for the uniform man to pick up. At about three months of age, Barker began to bark. His barking would escalate into a loud howl joined by his siblings. It was useless to try and silence them. When they finished their little tune, they would stop.

Digger, our lab with hound-like features, dug holes for the sheer pleasure of seeing the dirt fly. I've seem him almost disappear into a hole he was digging. Unless you noticed the dirt flying out of the hole, you wouldn't know he was there. I told my husband our yard looked like a war zone with the holes where Digger had tried to catch a mole. Often times he approached me with a cake of dried dirt still piled on top of his moist black nose. Occasionally I have stepped in one of his holes which landed me face first on the ground or sprawled out in a position I would not call ladylike.

One would think that three dogs would be a gracious plenty. At least that is what my husband thought. It's kind of like having one of those good/bad pleasures. You know, like having your children grow up and leave home. It's good that you don't have to clean up behind them anymore but you miss the mess they always made. Dogs are like that too. It was a continuous chore cleaning the front yard of the objects the dogs dragged up from the highway like deer hides, McDonald's happy meals, hubcaps, little bags of marijuana, or newspapers. At least you thought it was a newspaper. It was hard to tell all shredded like it was. The dogs had matured and grown out of that drag-everything-up puppy stage. We had calmed down for awhile. Then came Jennie.

One Sunday afternoon as my husband lay sleeping after having worked a night shift, a white pickup pulled into the driveway and the driver blew the horn. I didn't want my husband to wake up so I hurried out to greet the visitors. It turned out to be our neighbors up the road. One of the guys reached into the back of the pickup and picked up a puppy, golden in color wearing a red collar. He asked, "Is this your puppy? We found her running along the highway."

"No, it's not my puppy," I quickly replied.

I'm thinking to myself. *This is the most adorable little puppy. How could anyone throw such a sweet little puppy out? She will get hit by a car if she doesn't stay out of the highway.*

"Do you want me to see if I can find her owner?" I asked the guys.

They nodded in affirmation and as I think back, that was probably the fastest exit I have ever seen. The guys had handed me the puppy and before I had finished saying "owner" they had cranked their pickup and were halfway out the driveway.

What had I done? I had just accepted another dog without giving it a second thought. I knew it would be hard finding the owner and even if I found him or her it would be even harder to get the owner to admit ownership.

At least my husband was still asleep and I would try desperately to find the owner. Picture this. I'm still holding the puppy, her little body dangling from my hands. The dust had not yet settled from my fast exiting neighbors. As I turn around, the first thing I see is my husband standing at the front door looking at me. I felt like a kid who had just been caught with her hand in the cookie jar.

"I told them I would try and find the owner," I yelled to my husband.

"Sure," was all he said.

I did canvas the neighborhood but as I had expected, no one would accept ownership. My husband later put a seal on dogs.

"No more dogs!" he said.

I got the message. And I'm not even going to tell how we ended up with Oopsie, Pooka, Joobie, Indie, Crowie, Dieffenbachia, Delton, and Longfellow.

Scriptures tell the story of a poor man named Lazarus (Luke 16:19-26). This man was not only poor but he was sick. He had sores all over his body. He was poor, sick, and hungry. His existence was dependent upon the crumbs from a rich man's table and he had to beg for those. His plot in life was to lay at this rich man's gate waiting for a handout. Can you imagine the loneliness this poor beggar must have endured? Notice in verse 21 of Luke 16, "…the dogs came and licked his sores." Dogs were ministering to this sick man. I can just imagine they were a great comfort to this man's lonely existence. Why did God have to send dogs to do a man's job? Because man was in his big house, wearing his fine purple, with no financial worries. He was self absorbed thinking only of himself and oblivious to others in need around him.

Dogs are no respecter of people. Unless trained otherwise, dogs give their masters unconditional love. It doesn't matter to them if your clothes are wrinkled, if your hair is tangled, if your socks don't match, or if you have a pimple on the end of your nose. They love you just the way you are. We could all take a lesson in love from our dog friends.

Chapter 5
Birdie

Birdie had been passed down by so many owners that I don't think he even knew who his original owner was. Anyone who has ever owned a Quaker parrot knows that these birds demand attention. He came to me from a friend of my niece. I was unfamiliar with this type bird and when I said "yes, I'll take him," I did not know what I was getting myself into.

From the moment he was brought into my home, he established right off that he was the boss. "Good Birdie!" he screeched all day, every day, and all day long. He came with his own vocabulary. He knew other words and would not say them no matter how much I coaxed him in front of other people. If the visitors left, he would talk a blue streak.

"Go for a walk."

"Peek-a-boo."

"Want a scratch."

Try and carry on a normal conversation around him and he would drown you out with his squawking. "Bad Birdie!" I told him. He quickly replied, "Good Birdie!"

One particular afternoon, I was depressed. These were the months after my mother's death and I had very little to cheer me. My niece had spent the night with me and after she left to return to her home, my heart felt so empty. I was sitting in my bedroom sipping a cup of Earl Grey. I needed to get up and go to the office. I needed to get back into my regular routine. But my body would not move.

"Ha ha ha, hee hee hee, eeeeha ha ha ha, hee hee hee!"

Laughter was coming from the dining room.

"Ha ha ha, ha ha ha. Hee hee hee!"

It was Birdie. He was laughing. He not only had two laughs but he had several laughs. It sounded like a party. Evidently he had combined all the different laughs of his former owners. This went on for a full five or ten minutes. As I sat in my chair, tears began to roll down my face. These were tears of laughter. I laughed uncontrollably. I laughed freely. I was releasing all the sorrow built up inside. Afterwards, I felt great. Laughter was definitely the best medicine for me at that moment.

After Elijah the prophet confronted Ahab with a prophecy that no rain would fall in the land for three years, he hid himself by a brook named Cherith (1 Kings 17:1-9). God instructed him to hide there and he did until the brook dried up. During this time God sent ravens to feed Elijah. The ravens brought him bread and flesh in the morning, and bread and flesh in the evening (vs. 6). God used ravens to minister to the needs of Elijah.

Do you think Elijah ever wondered what would happen if the ravens did not show up? I think not. Sometimes people tell us things that they don't mean. "I'll see you this afternoon," they might say and thy never show up. "I'll call you tomorrow," and they never do. People can be undependable. Some lie. God needed something dependable. Elijah's life depended on it. The ravens never failed him. The ravens never failed because they were serving a God who never fails.

God can use a bird in a mighty way to feed a prophet or He can use a bird in a small way to cheer up a depressed soul. Either way the birds were ministers of an all powerful God.

Chapter 6
Happy

I had just sat down to the dining table to eat a hamburger. It had all the fixings, even a large slice of onion which I would never have added if I thought I was going to have company within the next few hours. These were the years I refer to as BM, before marriage. I was just about to take my first bite when I heard a knock at the door. Immediately my salivary glands went into remission. I reluctantly made my way to the door and opened it. There stood my brother holding a large grocery sack.

"Do you want what I have in here?" was his greeting.

Thinking it might be a large container of ice cream to go along with my delicious hamburger that awaited me, I said with a smile, "Sure."

My brother set the sack on the floor and I began to think then that it wasn't anything edible. Gradually he opened the sack and I peeped inside to see a little brown puppy. It lay quietly at the bottom of the sack. My brother had found it along a deserted gravel road.

It was the middle of November. In September I had lost my beloved Eleanor of thirteen years. She had succumbed to heart worms and I told myself I would never ever, have another dog. There I stood looking into the sack at the fuzzy little puppy and I felt my resolve weakening. To add to the situation, the little puppy was injured.

After my brother left, I immediately started cleaning the puppy's wounds. She had two large holes in her back. In a few weeks her injuries had healed and she had turned into a fuzzy little teddy bear. As with any healthy animal, she was a bundle of energy. Since nothing was known of her pedigree, it was interesting to see her grow into a big chocolate lab.

My nephew named her. Every opportunity we had to be together, we would go on hiking expeditions. We took the puppy along on these trips. She at times would get excited and circle us four or five times in an ecstatic run. My nephew would say, "She's having one of her happy spells." So we eventually named her "Happy."

Happy was everything you wanted in a dog. She was loving, loyal, happy and intelligent. I talked to her lots and I think she understood more than I realized. She could recognize my tone of voice and knew when I was serious or just kidding around. She could sense my mood and knew when to be calm or energetic. She was my companion and friend until I married. Then I had two friends. She adapted quite well to my married life especially when we moved to the farm.

The first three days at our new home, she barked nonstop. I guess she would have kept on barking except her voice gave out and then the only thing that came out was a little squeak. Eventually she settled down and grew to love the farm as I did. She had an entire pond she could call her own and she made full use of it.

My husband had a St. Bernard that lived with his parents on the farm. Because of his behavior of running off at times, he had to remain chained. I had reservations about introducing Happy to Tank because Tank weighed over a hundred pounds and Happy was probably fifty pounds at most. My concerns were futile because at their first encounter, Happy danced in front of Tank and the two looked like little puppies playing with one another.

It was this same joy each time Happy and Tank met up. One morning as I walked Happy, we made our usual trip by Tank who remained chained. Happy did her little dance in front of Tank and he ran with her. I don't know where my mind was at that particular moment but before I knew it, Happy had made several trips around me with Tank in pursuit. The big chain that held Tank was wrapped around me and I hit the ground harder than any football player. I carried the bruise, shaped like a large chain, on the back of my legs for weeks. Nothing else was hurt but my pride.

We had a jogging trail through the wooded area of our farm. Happy liked to run along with me. Once she made her way a few yards ahead of me and stopped in my path. I scolded her for blocking my path until I realized she had placed herself between me and a very large moccasin snake. Afterwards, I paid more attention to her warnings. She was to do this same protective act two more times in her lifetime.

I knew Happy was sick. The veterinarian had diagnosed heartworms about a year prior to her death. We have a special room we call the vet room where we keep our sick animals. I checked on Happy every two hours even through the night of her last week. Each time I entered the room, her eyes met mine and she wagged her tail. She never failed to recognize me even to the point of death. All my animals have a special place in my heart.

I cried for three months after Happy died. She taught me so much. Never did I dream that the gift my brother handed me in a paper sack would be a little puppy that would grow into a beautiful chocolate lab that would give to me the gift of happiness.

Chapter 7
Jack

Owning goats was a new experience for my husband and me. We were told it was the best way to get rid of briars and undergrowth which we needed at the time. We purchased four goats when they were three months old, two males and two females. When the male goats grew into adulthood they developed a strong, musky odor. When I say strong, I mean an odor that would stop you in your tracks and send you in the opposite direction in a run. It was obvious that we didn't need two male goats, so we found a nice home for one. After our goat family became large enough, we found a home for the other male goat.

When our first kid was born, we sent birth announcements to our family saying, "A New Kid on the Block." Many kids came along but none as sweet as Jack. Jack was one of triplets born to his mother Bo Peep. One of the triplets was born dead, one was accepted by the mother and there was Jack, rejected by his mother. She mourned over her dead baby, adored her second kid, but would have nothing to do with Jack.

I was determined that Jack was not going to die on the cold wet ground outside so I bundled him up, brought him inside, and placed him in a clothes basket. He was no larger than a small cat, much too small for a baby goat to live. My mother-in-law, a retired registered nurse, took one look at him and shook her head. "I just don't think he's going to make it. He's much too small."

Using a medicine dropper, I tried to give Jack some milk, just a few drops every few hours. His cold wet body began to dry out and his eyes began to brighten. I continued using the medicine dropper and suddenly, it dawned on Jack that he had to suckle to get more milk. After that realization, Jack couldn't get enough milk. In a few days he was nursing from a bottle. He was soon standing and asking for a bottle, "Baaa, "he would say. A clothes basket made the perfect little play pen. So Jack lived in our house until he outgrew the clothes basket.

My husband built Jack a small pen beside the larger goat pen. His sister Jill was larger than Jack but both were such small kids they could go in and out of the goat pen by simply stepping through the wire. Jack's mother still rejected him but Jill would go through the pen and play with Jack. I would often look out my window and see the kids playing all over the yard.

When Jack outgrew his youth, he was placed in the pen with the other goats. Not only did Jack's mother continue to reject him, but the other goats made sport of him. When it rained they would not let him in the goat house. When they ate they always butted him out of the way. Jack preferred human company to his own kind and I could understand why. He loved playing with the dogs and cats. It was not uncommon to see him chasing the cats around the yard.

Once I had raked a large pile of leaves to burn. I had watched the fire until I thought it safe to leave. Jack was such a part of the outside especially vying for attention like all the other animals that sometimes I didn't pay him much notice. It wasn't until I started smelling this awful strange smell that I looked back. Jack had walked right through the burning leaves. He never said a word. I examined his feet to find all four with singed hair. From then on I paid a little more attention to him as he followed me outside.

Jack grew up to be as big, if not bigger, than the rest of the herd. He was bigger than his sister Jill. Despite his size he was still ostracized by his family. When Jack was twelve years old, he broke his leg. I visited the vet for advice. I described the break and its location on the leg. When I told him Jack's age, he shook his head in a manner that said *don't bother trying to help him.* Nevertheless, I picked up an antibiotic and pain killer and when my husband came in from work, we set the break. During the next six weeks I gave Jack lots of TLC and pears. Jack's leg mended and we had the privilege of his company for three more years.

Jack outlived his family. He was an example of endurance. When the odds were against him, he beat the odds. I always thought of him as my spoiled little kid. To this day I cannot see a pear that it doesn't remind me of Jack.

Chapter 8
Fossy

Fossy was the first fox I had the privilege of raising. When my cousin brought her by she was just a baby, probably less than six week old. My cousin worked at a wood yard which shipped logs by barge to a paper mill. When his loader turned a rather large log over he saw a fox run from under it. He crawled down from his loader and found two baby foxes. The log had crushed one but the other was still alive. The mother disappeared.

When my cousin presented me with the baby, I thought it was the cutest little kit I'd ever seen, small, slim with a pointed nose. He had it wrapped in an old shirt, the only thing he could find at the time. He said, "I hope she doesn't growl," as he handed the little creature to me. *What's a little growl*, I thought.

I took the kit inside my house and placed it in a large pet taxi. I took several towels and made a warm bed for her. She was quiet and I was excited at the chance to raise her. I was impressed at her calmness and thought she would make the ideal pet. I couldn't wait for my husband to come home from work to see her.

When my husband finally arrived that afternoon, I was excited to show him my new pet. As he peeped into the pet taxi, all he could see was a set of very sharp teeth and the most voracious growl that resonated throughout the house. I almost dropped the pet taxi. She had come out of the shock she evidently was in. From then on every piece of food and water I placed into the taxi was greeted with that awful growl.

My husband put on a pair of welding gloves to remove the little critter so I could clean the taxi. My thoughts of holding a cute little cuddly puppy vanished by day's end.

While my husband was away at work, I thought on how I could tame this little creature. *Maybe she just needs a larger area to run around in. Sure, why hadn't I thought of that before?* So I took Fossy to our upstairs apartment which had lots of space. She could run around up there to her heart's content.

I placed the pet taxi in the middle of the room. Before opening the door I placed a large bowl of food and water in the kitchenette. I positioned myself on the floor to observe her as she checked out her new surroundings. She gradually eased out of the pet taxi and slowly checked out her environment. She went slowly along the walls into the kitchen. *Good*, I thought, *she's checking out the food.* Wrong!

She found a tiny hole beside the hot water heater which only led to the small space, about four inches, under the cabinets. Unfortunately it ran the length of the counter top and there was no way to get to this space except through that tiny hole. I waited for a long time and she never came out. *Now what had I done?*

I left her there that day and checked on her the next morning. She had come out during the night and eaten her food. At least I knew she was alright. This went on for a week. I was determined to catch her again and sat vigil one night. After about three hours, I heard her scratching but she must have known I was there and she never came out.

The next night I brought a book and positioned myself on the floor so I had a good view of the hole by the hot water heater and the food bowls. It took four hours before the hunger overcame her fear of me. She eased out, took a few bites of food, and then hurried back into her self made den.

I could rest knowing that she was eating but the area under the cabinets would not hold her for long if she grew at all. She could not live her life in the apartment. She had to be caught and placed in another environment.

My husband set a live trap for her. We placed her food inside it and waited. She quit eating. She was smarter than we thought.

"We've got to get her out of there," my husband said.

On his first off day, my husband brought his welding gloves and a large crow bar upstairs. He began ripping boards off the cabinets. Pulling nails and ripping boards made a terrible sound. He finally made it to the last partition under the cabinets and there she was. He put on his gloves and grabbed the growling little furry ball and placed her in the pet taxi. She was then transported to the habitat. The habitat had a pool, hollow log, rocks, dens and plenty of hiding places all surrounded by wire. She was released and went straight into the hollow log.

During the next few weeks, I took her food to her and she would come out and eat. I slowly eased my hand to her and she began to let me pet her. She could climb the wire and I always felt a little uneasy when she climbed it while I was in with her. She would sit on top of one of the squirrel cages and watch me from above.

When I took the dogs for their morning run, she was always watchful. I think she would have joined them had I let her. Our latest dog drop-off came just a month before we received Fossy. We had named him Pooka and although Pooka and Fossy were close to the same age, Pooka was much bigger. I let Pooka in the habitat with me and it was as if I had united a family. The two played together like two little puppies. This became an every day ritual.

Fossy grew into a beautiful little gray fox. It was liberation time. I felt that she was old enough now to survive in the wild. I opened the door to the habitat and watched as she discovered it was open. She slowly walked over the yard and into the woods.

Every night for the next two weeks I sat her food bowl out by the edge of the woods. I could spot her using a flashlight. Her red eyes would shine and make their way to the bowl. I'd tell her all she missed that day by being away. She would eat and quickly disappear. She gradually stopped coming and I knew she had made the transition well. She had returned to the wild.

Chapter 9
Quack, Quack

When my cousin brought them to me, he said, "I think I have you a pair."

They were just two little balls of black and yellow fluff. I don't know how he could tell he had given me a male and female baby duck. He was right though and the pair grew into adults and produced many more little ducks and those ducks grew and more ducks were produced and so on.

Since we had a large pond, I thought the ducks would enjoy swimming around on it rather than parking their little feathers so they could watch the back door and beat the cats to their food. The cats found them quite intimidating and allowed their feathered friends to eat what was appropriated to them. The trouble is that cats are nibblers. They like to have their food pans full of food but like to nibble at it and make it last all day or all night. Ducks are early risers and the first thing they do upon awakening is to run and check the cat pans.

Have you ever been awakened from a deep sleep by a jack hammer? Well, I haven't either but I can only imagine it sounds a lot like a bunch of duck beaks pounding on large metal pans. We have twelve cats so we buy large pans to accommodate them. When old White Neck (that is what we call one mallard with a large white neck band) leads his flock of followers to the porch, there is no more sleep for me.

I tried several tactics to break them from eating out of the cat pans. I threw my shoes at the ducks. They flew about six feet off the porch and laughed at me. I tried throwing water on them. *What was I thinking when I did that?* Ducks live for water. I tried loud noises like hollowing loud enough to wake my neighbors a half mile away. Nothing seemed to work until by accident one morning I had a black umbrella in my hand. When I stepped out on to the porch and pressed the button that released the umbrella, the ducks took off flying and didn't land until they reached the pond. A few mornings of the black umbrella treatment cured the early morning jackhammer, for awhile at least.

A lot in life has to be learned by *a posteriori* (experience) like which end of a duck to hold. I had to learn the hard way. We had a duck nesting and the little ones were hatching out. I wanted to lift the duck to count the little ones so I'd know how many to keep up with once she left the nest. I lifted the duck with her rear pointed toward me. Never do that. She had been sitting on her nest all day with the babies and hadn't had a chance to *go* yet. When I lifted her up there was a black explosion. I was covered in duck poop from my head to below my belt. I dropped the duck and staggered away spitting and gagging as I went. Somewhere between the duck nest and the house, I slung my blouse off. Lesson well learned.

Ducks are easily spoiled like most farm animals. I felt sorry for one crippled duck who allowed the horse to stand on her foot until it broke. I started feeding her by hand and she expected it from then on. When I fed the others, they ate as fast as I threw it to the ground. She would stand looking straight up at me quacking for me to hand her some. Of course, I would and this became the norm. I named her Cripple Duck.

I remember the first year the pond froze over. I had my bucket of corn but couldn't find the ducks. I finally had to walk to the pond and eyed them on the opposite side. They were swimming in circles in an area about ten feet in diameter. By doing this, they had kept that part of the pond from freezing.

I quacked. That is how I call the ducks to come to me. They acknowledged my quack with their quacks and kept swimming in circles. They saw me and knew they had to get to me but didn't know how. I guess White Neck realized he was quite hungry after swimming in circles all night and had better make a move if he was to get his breakfast. He flapped his wings and landed on the solid ice. Others followed him. Soon there was a line of ducks following each other en route to me. I guess some were hungrier than others because they began to fly toward me. I was standing on the bank by a long pier. As the first duck landed, I realized about the same time he realized that he really didn't know how to land on ice. He slid about six feet and hit one of the posts holding up the pier. Others would land and bounce back and forth from tail feathers to head trying to maintain a balance. Their webbed feet were like skis and they had to balance themselves to keep from falling. One skied right on into the bank, walked up the bank and started eating his breakfast. They were slipping and sliding into each other. The few that decided to walk across the pond were just as funny. Their little webbed feet would slip out from under them and they'd hit the ice then scurry to get back up and walk faster. They all finally made it safely.

I was laughing so hard when I told my husband about them that the next time the pond iced over, we went together to the pond to feed the ducks. That time I took my camcorder and recorded the same scenario all over again.

During mating season the ducks can be cruel to one another. Since Cripple Duck couldn't get around as fast as the others, this made her an easy target for the males. She began to hide out on the other side of the pond to get a little relief from the amorous males. I have to assume that this was also the reason for her broken wing, which I discovered one morning. Now Cripple Duck had to contend with the broken foot and the broken wing. But still she could get around and still liked to hang out on the back side of the pond. I made a special point to feed her every morning and evening on the back side of the pond. All I had to do was *Quack* and she would hop out from her hiding place and eat.

When the mating season was over, she began to come back to the house where we feed the rest of the ducks. I began to notice that her wing was looking worse, yet she still managed to make the trip to the house for meals.

One morning, my husband was making the rounds and he found Cripple Duck by the water's edge. Her head was bobbing up and down. She was dying. My husband brought her to the vet room and summoned me.

"If you want to see her alive, you'd better hurry," he said.

I hurried to the vet room. Cripple Duck was fading fast. She looked at me one last time. I sat and talked to her. I told her what a good duck and good companion she had been to me and that I would miss her. I then told her that she could leave us now. With those words, she lay down and died. I always believe that she held on to life so that I could tell her goodbye. She knew how important that was to me.

Chapter 10
Hidie

It has been the practice of the cats to bring gifts to me and leave them on the mat at my back door. This practice has been going on as long as I've had cats. These gifts can range from pieces of rodents to the entire body. I've become quite adept at identifying small rodents by their internal organs.

One such morning I saw a small intestine on the mat. It appeared to be one from either a rat or a chipmunk. As I stepped onto the porch, I saw a short section of tail which I knew to be that of the chipmunk.

I knew that once the cats found a den of chipmunks, they would hunt them until all were killed. Most of the time, as with our cats that are well fed, the cat will play with their prey rather than eat it. Such play usually leaves the prey injured or dying. Occasionally, there have been times I have captured the prey before the cats had a chance to hurt it.

After the morning I first saw the chipmunk organs, I had a feeling I would see more. One such chipmunk was rescued by my husband before the cats killed it. My husband left it in a hamster cage for me.

I observed the chipmunk for three days to make sure it was not injured. It seemed to be in perfect health. I could not release it near our house for fear the cats would catch it again. I could not release it any farther away, because the creature would not have time to fill its den with winter nuts and other foods for the winter. I had no choice but to keep it through the winter and release it the next spring when food would be in supply again.

Chipmunks make their homes in the earth in dens they dig usually around old stumps and in areas where water will not flood their dens. As I thought about a winter home for the chipmunk, I had a brainstorm. I had an aquarium not being used. So I went to work making a suitable habitat for the chipmunk. I put a layer of dirt on the bottom. I found a piece of driftwood and such a pretty little piece it was. My husband bored a hole in the piece of wood large enough for me to fill with soil and plant a small oak tree. So I placed the driftwood on the layer of dirt with the little tree growing out from it. Next, I arranged numerous rocks around the wood. In one corner I piled an assortment of nuts and placed a bowl of water in the opposite corner. Then I picked up a handful of maple leaves. There were red, yellow, and orange leaves and I made sure I had an assortment. These, I pilled to one side of the aquarium. As I looked at the little habitat, I thought it would make a fine home for my winter guest. It was an aesthetic masterpiece.

The aquarium was in my office so I left it there thinking it would be a nice place to keep the chipmunk during the winter months. After the completion of the magnum opus, I carefully placed the chipmunk in his new home and left him for the night to adjust to his new abode.

The next morning I was anxious to see how the chipmunk was adjusting. As I opened the door to my office, my mouth flew open. The nice little habitat, so meticulously constructed, looked as if a little tornado had hit it. The little tree had been gnawed down and was on top of the leaves which had been piled to look like a teepee. The nuts were scattered and water bowl turned over. The dirt had been scratched and piled. I had to laugh a little. The chipmunk had certainly made himself at home.

For the next week, the chipmunk would come from his hiding place under the leaves and sit on the drift wood. I always made sure he had plenty of nuts and noticed that he took a liking to apple. Every day at lunch, I would save him a slice of my apple. I was concerned about the moisture content inside the aquarium. He had turned his water bowl over the first night and it had soaked the bottom. I noticed moisture on the sides of the aquarium from this water spill so I started leaving the top off a few hours each day to help dry it out. The top of the aquarium was just a board that I could easily slide off. Sometimes, I'd remove the board or just crack it a bit. Never, did I leave it cracked when I wasn't there. I knew how quick chipmunks could be.

He would often come out and sit on his driftwood and eat his apple as I sat behind my desk working. He did not like the idea of me getting to close to his habitat and would hide under the leaves when I approached. So I learned to observe him from afar.

One morning I had so much work to do and I was running so far behind that I only took a five minute lunch break. I was so preoccupied with my work that I forgot to close the top to the aquarium. It's odd that I thought about it about the time I was taking a bite of apple. I rushed back to the office and peered into the aquarium. The chipmunk was gone.

To understand the nightmare I faced, one would have to see my office. I have a back wall of book shelves loaded to capacity with books. I have a desk with stacks of books and magazines piled on top. I have copiers, computers and a thousand places a chipmunk could hide. I thought to myself. *Surely he will have to show himself to find food to eat. And I'll catch him when he does.*

By afternoon, I had rigged up the aquarium. I placed it on the floor, propped the lid up with a stick, tied a long string to the stick and ran the string into the next room. I placed an apple slice inside the aquarium. Then I sat outside the office holding the string in one hand and trying to be as quiet and motionless as possible. I sat as long as my arthritic joints would allow me. No sign of the chipmunk. My husband was waiting supper. I had to go.

The next morning I found the apple peel by my desk. The chipmunk had feasted on the apple and left me a token. He had also removed all the leaves from the aquarium. That meant that he was building a nest somewhere in the office. *But where?*

I placed another apple slice inside the aquarium and more leaves and took my position outside the office, with string in hand. About an hour into the post, the telephone rang. Oops! I had forgotten to unplug the phone. I answered the phone which required me to leave the office for about ten minutes. When I returned, the apple was gone and the leaves.

How did he know I had left the office? Did he smell me? Could he feel the vibrations of my feet as I walked across the floor? Somehow he knew.

I returned with more leaves and an apple slice. Also, I brought back with me a can of Lysol spray which I sprayed the office with to confuse his sense of smell. *Now I had him*, so I thought.

Another day wasted. Maybe he had a routine. Eat at a certain time, bathe afterwards, and so on. I asked my husband to wake me when he left for work at 4:30, not my usual waking time. I'd spend the day as a sentinel until that little rascal showed himself.

I arrived at the office before sunrise. I dressed in camouflage. I took my position outside the door. This time, I lay down with my eyes fixed on the aquarium and with my hand holding onto the string which would spring the trap which awaited the surreptitious little pest. By noon, there had been no sighting and I was starving. I quickly went home to eat a bite and returned only to find the apple gone and the leaves missing. And by my desk was an apple peel. On my hands and knees, I followed a tiny trail of leaves. They led to the bookcases behind my desk.

I spent the afternoon canceling all my appointments for the rest of the week. I realized that I was working with a mastermind, a Houdini, a genius.

While I was at my desk rearranging my schedule, he boldly gnawed on a pecan not two feet from me, under my bookcase, but secure as if there was a concrete wall between the two of us.

The next morning I took my time. I had my coffee. I then set to work moving all the books off the first unit of shelves. I stacked them in the middle of the office. Then I eased the set of shelves out enough to where I could get behind them. No chipmunk.

I went to work on the second unit of shelves, placing all the magazines on the floor. It was beginning to look like a maze. Still no chipmunk.

I bravely tackled the third and last unit of shelves. Now my office was so cluttered that I could not move about in it without knocking over a stack of magazines or books. I had a yardstick which I ran under the bottom of the shelves since I was squeezed between the unit and the back wall. The units were partitioned at the base so I had to run the yardstick under three different sections on each unit. On my last section as I kneeled, sandwiched between the wall and the shelves, running the yardstick under the unit, out came the furry little creature. He made a mad dive up my leg and over my shoulder and was lost in the maze of books, magazines and furniture.

I squeezed from my position behind the shelves and started the search all over again. I found him in the corner of the office and as quickly as I did he was behind the shelves again. I'd run him out from behind the shelves and into the jungle of books he would go. A few hours into this game and I was about to annihilate the little scoundrel. By evening I was worn to a frazzle. Upon arriving home from work, my husband took one look at me and his eyes told it all, *who is this crazy woman?* I told him of my day which was redundant because my appearance told it all. With his help, we managed to catch the little scalawag and place him back into the aquarium and place the aquarium in a building far away from my office.

I have determined that the little troublemaker is a female. I came to this conclusion because every time I put leaves in her habitat, she rearranges it. She has done more digging, moving and rearranging in that one little complex than most rodents do in a lifetime. She and I have come to an understanding. I will feed her, which includes a slice of apple each day, and provide her a comfortable home until the arrival of spring, if she will only behave. So far, the arrangement has worked out well.

Chapter 11
The Otter

It's odd how we note events in our lives after catastrophes. It's probably because they make such an indelible mark on our lives that they seem too impossible to forget. Like the blizzard of 1993, the tornado of 1998, hurricane Ivan in 2004 and five hurricanes in 2005. Each of these events left our farm with damage to trees and buildings, creating massive piles of limbs and debris. My back hurts just thinking about the cleanup.

There is still visible damage on our property left by hurricane Ivan. I remember how tiring the weeks of cleanup left me. My body ached during those weeks and I dreaded getting up in the mornings. Meanwhile, the regular chores of feeding all the critters and walking the dogs continued on schedule.

One morning as I was walking the dogs around the pond, I noticed a movement in the pond. At first, I thought it was just a log. The winds from hurricane Ivan had left many limbs scattered throughout the pond. Most had floated to the edges of the pond but this particular limb, it seemed, still floated in the middle.

I glanced at it again and it was gone. *My eyes are playing tricks on me*, I thought. I had to admit that my mind was engrossed in the chores which still lay ahead of me. Also, I was physically tired from weeks of using muscles I was not accustomed to using. *Maybe I had just seen a reflection in the water.*

The dogs continued their running and sniffing. They did not see the disappearing log in the pond, thus I was more convinced that I had not seen anything either. About that time, the log appeared again and disappeared just as quickly. This sighting brought my long stride to a halt. I stood at the pond's edge and watched. It appeared again. I couldn't tell if it was one object or two. It appeared to be a mini Leviathan. It moved about the pond, popping up and disappearing. It was a long animal of some sort, one that I had never seen before.

I quickly finished the dog walk and placed my camera in my pocket. I had to slip through the woods away from the dogs to keep them from following me to get back to the pond. I knew the dogs had probably not seen the animal or else they would have swam out to it and checked it out. Also, it would be an impossible task to get a closer look at the animal with the dogs around me.

I approached the pond as quietly as I could. Easing my way to the water's edge, I kneeled and searched the pond for any sign of movement. About half way along the pond's dam, a log lay half submerged in the water. The log's greater end rose from the water and rested on the bank. Vines were wrapped around it still holding on to their yellow ochre leaves. Just out of the water, on this log, lay the little creature. I could see its long sleek body. It appeared to be sun bathing.

I had to get closer. I had an idea of what it was but I had to get a closer look because I had never, in all my life, seen a real live one. I slowly made my way to the animal. The dam was bare and there was nothing I could hide behind. The animal saw me and slid into the water.

I walked to the log and sat on the ground behind it. I remained there until I saw the creature again. It was swimming, disappearing and reappearing in the water in a rhythmic motion. Each time it popped its head out of the water, it had its eyes on me.

I continued to sit and observe. The creature swam a long time and seemed to want to rest. He wanted to rest on *his* log. Of all the places in and around the pond, he wanted the spot on the log. By then I had determined that the little creature was a river otter.

He had a dark, slick body that looked black in the water. His ears and eyes were small and his whiskers were white. The longer I kept my position, the closer he swam to the log. Soon he was at the log and I could hear his grunts and low growl.

As he approached the log, I began to talk to him. He responded with his little grunts. The more I talked, the more he responded. He finally positioned himself on the log but hid behind the leaves wrapped around the log. He would peek out from behind the leaves at me. I just kept on talking to him.

I sat there on the ground hardly moving except to position the camera for a shot now and then. I explained to the little otter that if he allowed me to get one good shot of him, I would leave him alone and he could rest on the log as long as he wanted. He peeked at me and growled.

My camera is not the best in the world and I missed several good shots of him peeking through the leaves. But true to my word, I thought I had at least one good picture of him, so I left. I had sat on the ground over two hours and that was about the limit my body could take.

When I returned to the pond that afternoon, I saw no sign of the otter. He had returned from whence he came. In my twenty years of living on the farm, this was the first and only time I had ever seen an otter. All I could figure was that when hurricane Ivan had moved through our area dropping massive amounts of rain and changing our landscape forever, it had disturbed the otter's habitat also.

I always felt like the otter was a gift God had sent to cheer me. I know that after my encounter with one of His little creatures, I left with a renewed spirit. I was able to finish the dreaded job of cleanup. I can still see his little pixie face peeking at me through the leaves and hear his soft little growl as if he was saying; *all is right with the world.*

Chapter 12
Ramses I

When the lady gave us the sheep, we really didn't know what we were getting in for. They were corralled into a barn. From there, my husband loaded them into the back of a pickup with a camper shell attached. It was five Jacob sheep, one ram and four ewes, in bad need of shearing, or so we thought.

Our two eighteen year old mustangs must have thought they were the ugliest creatures they'd ever seen or the scariest. They stared first at the sheep and then ran. They even made a few new gates in our old fences, ones that we didn't need. Having been raised around miniature horses, the sheep wanted to be near the horses in their strange new environment. The horses, having never seen a sheep before, wanted nothing to do with the ugly creatures. It was close to a week before the horses stopped running from the sheep.

Soon after we unloaded the sheep, we noticed that the ram had a serious problem with his horns. One horn was curved and growing into the side of his face. The curve in the horn passed right in front of his left eye before it entered the side of his face. In order to see out of that eye, the ram had to drop his head and look upward. Parasites had already infested the area where the horn grew into his face and the poor ram fought the flies continually and kept his head buried in the ground when sleeping. He looked miserable all the time and I'm sure he was.

We quickly made an appointment with our veterinarian to have the ram's horn cut from the side of his face. The surgery was successful and immediately we could see the ram's bright eyes. He could look at us straight on without having to tilt his head. The hole in his face quickly healed and the ram strutted everywhere he went. It was good to see him feeling better. We named him Ramses I. We even sent his veterinarian a card saying, "Thank you for the extreme makeover."

It didn't take the sheep long to adjust to their new surroundings. A little feed can work wonders. Soon they were begging for handouts like all the other critters on the farm.

A few months later, as I was making my rounds feeding all the animals, I stopped at the gate leading to the sheep pasture. My mind likes to travel when I do mundane chores and it was far away as I struggled with the gate latch trying to get it open. I am usually serenaded by roosters crowing, hens cackling, ducks quacking, horses neighing, dogs barking, cats meowing and now the sheep baaing. This particular morning I heard the sound of a soft little baa. *Baaaaaa.*

I was brought back to the present by the sound of the little baa. My mind was trying to process the sound. It was telling me that I had never heard that sound before. Yet it sounded so familiar. My eyes took over then and started searching for the sound. They scanned the pasture and the group of sheep standing, looking straight toward me and wondering when they would ever get their feed.

Then I spotted the little baa-maker. It was so small standing among the large sheep. It was a baby lamb. I stood at the gate just looking at this precious little creature. Tears rolled down my cheeks. *Baaaaaa.* It sounded again.

My husband and I had no idea any of our sheep were expecting. Their thick wool was a good cover. We had three more lambs born that February. Some of my most enjoyable afternoons were spent lying on the grass, watching the lambs play. They ran fast, leaped high in the air, and jumped. They chased one another. They were curious little animals, chasing the ducks and the cats.

The psalmist said, "The mountains skipped like rams, and the hills like lambs" (Psalm 114:4). Just watching the sheep and lambs has brought the Scriptures, especially portions of the Psalms, alive to me. I thought about

David in his night watches as he tended the sheep. He had to have pictured his sheep as he wrote the Psalms.

We were pleased to learn that Ramses had no residual effects from his surgery and I guess he had to show us that he didn't. He was just as proud of the lambs as we were.

Chapter 13
Holly

We acquired Holly in the usual way. Someone dumped her out at the end of our driveway. I stepped out one morning to feed the cats and I could hear the loudest *meow* coming from the direction of the driveway. As I followed the sound of the meow, I found myself standing, looking down at the skinniest, ugliest, little kitten I'd ever seen.

I picked the little flea bag up and took her to the vet room and gave her a good meal. It was hard to tell her age because of her malnutrition. She was probably in the range of four to six weeks of age.

With lots of food, TLC and worming, Holly turned into a pretty kitten. Se was vocal from that very first day I picked her up. It doesn't take long to spoil a cat, especially when you're giving her extra attention for her health.

Holly decided she didn't like the other ten cats we had and wanted to be an inside cat. Since she was such a terror to the other cats, she got her way.

We put her out at night but she lies on the porch watching the back door, waiting for the chance to come back inside. When I feed the cats in the mornings, she makes a quick entrance. She is content to stay inside all day and at night has to be shoved out again.

Holly has several meows. One says, *I'm hungry, feed me now*. Another meow says, *Scratch me under the chin or scratch me behind the ear*. And then there is that meow which says, *I'm sleeping, don't bother me*. But the most important meow is the one that says *I'm sick*.

One afternoon I rushed through the house to pick up something I had forgotten. I remember I was in a hurry and when I heard the *meow*, I mistook it for the *meow* that says, *I'm hungry, feed me now*. I told Holly that I'd be right back to feed her. I rushed on out and finished the project that seemed so important to me at the time.

It was an hour before I went back inside and I immediately knew that I'd erred. I spotted a trail of throw-up that led from the hallway all the way to the bathroom. As I was putting my cleaning supplies away and wondering to myself how a cat could hold that much food, I spotted another pile in my study.

I have Holly figured out now. She is bulimic, kind of. It's rooted in her childhood. She remembers being hungry as a kitten. Sometimes I see her just lying by the food bowl. She eats when she sees another cat passing by her. She thinks they are heading to the food bowl and she must get there first. She eats while I am preparing supper. She eats when I eat. She is a social eater. She eats all day long and it can't help but come back up.

The only time when Holly doesn't eat is when she sleeps. When she catches me reading a book, she hops into my lap and is content to lay there. Otherwise, she is on my bed with all four feet sticking straight up and eyes wide open, but sound asleep.

Chapter 14
Big Bird

We have a two acre pond on the farm. The level of water it maintains depends on the amount of rainfall we receive. Often times, I've seen it almost dry up. I wondered how any life could be left in it after such a long dry spell. But by the following spring, after a long wet winter, the pond would be alive again with tiny fish, turtles and all kinds of fauna and flora.

The pond is a haven for our domesticated mallards. They see a lot of visitors to the pond like coots, Canadian geese, wood ducks, and egrets and there is usually one great blue heron that makes its home at the pond.

For several years a great blue heron made the pond its haunt. He could be seen in the early mornings and the late afternoons standing in the pond's edge, watching, for frogs, fish or turtles, its principal food.

When we first moved to the farm, I was unknowledgeable about the aquatic wildlife. This was evident late one afternoon as I stood outside the house watching one of the cats. The cat was sitting looking up at me when I noticed the cat cringe and its eyes widen. It was staring past me when its countenance changed. Then I saw a shadow of a large winged creature pass over me. I heard an eerie squawk as I looked up. I probably scared the cat worse than the bird. I thought I'd seen a pterodactyl. I was to learn later that it was a great blue heron.

The heron hung around the pond for many years and we named him Big Bird. He was a pleasure to watch. One day I came home from work and found the bird caught in the fence. I often wondered if it had been in a fight with another heron invading his territory. He had probably struggled all day trying to free himself from the fence. With a pair of needle nose pliers, I cut the fence to free him. He was too badly injured to fly off. I placed him in the vet room. He died the next morning while I was out in thirty-two degree weather trying to catch him a fish.

After his death, I examined his body. I have never been as impressed with a bird as I was him. I measured his wing span, his height, the length of his bill and many more measurements which I have since misplaced. He was a magnificent bird. He earned a place in our pet cemetery and I made a marker for him with the name Big Bird.

Since Big Bird's demise, many great blues have taken up residence at the pond. Maybe some of those herons were Big Bird's descendents. I would like to think so anyway.

Chapter 15
Woody

On one of my afternoon walks with the dogs, I passed by a large oak tree. A noise caught my attention. When I found the source of the noise, I was surprised. It was a baby bird, sitting in the middle of a horse pod with ants crawling all over it. I quickly grabbed the little creature and began brushing and picking off the ants. The entire time I was doing the *de-anting*, the baby bird was squawking.

As I examined him, I could see that he didn't have all his feathers. He couldn't have flown to that location. I searched the oak for any sign of a nest. I saw none and neither did I see an adult bird. Usually, they fly around, trying to protect their babies, but not so with this case. I assumed that the little fellow had fallen out of his nest.

I found the little guy a safe place in the vet room. I knew he was probably hungry and possibly injured from the fall. I didn't hold much hope for his survival. Most abandoned baby birds do not thrive.

My husband was home that day sawing pine lumber on his sawmill. He saw me trying to find earthworms and pulled back the bark on one of the pines he was sawing and gathered about ten pine grubs. I started feeding the bird these grubs and he swallowed them as fast as I could put them in his mouth.

After I knew the baby bird had food in his stomach, I began to try and identify him. I determined that he was in the woodpecker family but what kind I couldn't tell because he didn't have all his feathers.

Then I researched all the wildlife materials I had and found a formula to feed woodpeckers. It consisted of a concoction of ground beef, dog food, turtle food, egg yolks, grit or sand and cottage cheese. The only ingredient I didn't have was the cottage cheese.

The next day I started feeding the little guy with the formula. He eagerly ate and then closed his eyes to let me know that he'd had enough. For the next two weeks I fed the bird the formula from sunrise to sunset, every one to two hours.

I'd place him in a parrot cage at night but during the day he had full range of the vet room. Once he started to fly, I cut a tree limb, mounted a flat board on the bottom and placed it in the vet room. He would climb the tree and hang on to it.

In his first attempts to fly, he would glide to the floor then walk over to me and climb up my legs and hang on to my shirt. I let him hang there because he was close and easy to feed in that position. Then he started venturing a bit farther up and something about my hair fascinated him. It sent chills up my spine so I'd remove him and place him back on his tree.

After about two weeks he began to reject his formula. I'd try to poke it down him and he'd sling it all over the floor and me. I began mixing earthworms, egg whites and grapes with the formula. He seemed to like the change.

He became more active in the vet room and would fly all around the room. He began climbing the tree and sticking a very long tongue out to taste or smell the bark. On the tip of the tongue was a sensor.

I placed several food items on the tree so he could learn to eat from the tree. One article about woodpeckers said that woodpeckers consume a large percentage of tree sap. I substituted honey water. The first time he tasted it is still vivid. I put a drop on the end of my finger and as he made his way up the tree tasting various foods, he came to my finger. Out came the long tongue, longer than his beak, and touched the end of my finger. The feel of the little woodpecker tongue touching my finger is a feeling I will cherish for a long time.

All my research stated that when the bird can gain altitude in flight, they can be released. Woody had been flying around the room and flying up and getting on top of the cabinets for several days. I knew he was ready to be released.

After feeding Woody a good breakfast, I took him to a wooded area on our land. I placed him on a sweet gum tree and watched him for twenty minutes. He inched his way up the tree, pecking at the bark as he went. He made adult sounds which he had never made inside the vet room. He went all the way up to the top of the tree and then flew over to a pine tree. That was the last time I saw Woody.

Woody knew what to do in the wild and I had a good feeling that he was going to be alright. Although I was happy for him, he left a big empty spot in my heart.

Chapter 16
Dennis

I guess by now it has been established that I walk the dogs every morning. These walks usually take us through a trail in the pines and around a two acre pond. Except for the extreme cold, stifling heat, high humidity, stormy weather, elevated pollen levels or winds gusting to near hurricane strength, these walks are usually enjoyable. On the pleasant days, I usually observe the fauna and flora on these walks.

I enjoy watching the bass and bream feed around the edges of the pond. A great blue heron is usually near or maybe a snipe or two. They usually take flight when they see the dogs coming. The pond contains numerous species of turtles; among these is the painted turtle.

The female turtle lays a clutch of eggs in the soil away from the pond. These clutches may contain as many as a dozen or more eggs. She leaves them to hatch on their own. After about ten or eleven weeks, the baby turtles hatch out and make their way to the pond. I often see these little hatchlings on their trip to the pond during my walks. When I see one, I usually pick it up and take it to the pond to keep it from being stepped on by the horses, goats or sheep.

One particular morning, I saw a little hatchling making its way through the sheep on its way to the pond. *This is dangerous*, I thought. So I picked the little fellow up and took him to the pond's edge and gently released him into the pond. It's always a pleasure to see them scoot away and disappear into the murky darkness of the pond. I watched as this little guy started to swim. He gave it all he had but only went in circles and then flipped upside down. I picked him up and examined him. I noticed that he looked at me kind of sideways but didn't think too much of it until I placed him in the water again. He swam around in circles and flipped upside down with his little yellow bottom brightly shining. I knew if the little guy couldn't keep himself upright that he wasn't going to live. He would drown if he couldn't flip himself. Besides, with his the yellow bottom of his shell shining, the blue heron would have him for a meal in no time.

This is how I ended up with a disabled turtle as a pet. I named him Dennis after the hurricane that passed through at the time I found him. He also reminded me of a hurricane as he spun around in the water.

When Dennis is picked up, he retreats to his shell. He looks perfectly normal in his shell. As he stretches his long neck out, his head tilts to one side. Also, the odd movement of his legs indicates his right side is impaired. This is why Dennis cannot keep his balance.

I bought Dennis a turtle habitat from the local pet store. It had a cute little plastic palm tree and a little red bridge that Denis could crawl over or hide under. Dennis cared noting for any of that. He was more interested in eating.

As Dennis grew, he needed a larger habitat. I bought a small aquarium and placed two rocks inside it. I then poured enough water to make it two inches in depth. In this amount of water, Dennis could swim around. His feet touched the bottom of the aquarium which enabled him to keep his balance. When he tired, he could crawl onto the rocks and rest.

One of the rocks I placed in the aquarium had a little point on the edge. I was sitting on the couch reading one day and kept hearing a bumping sound. I observed Dennis for awhile. He would crawl up onto his rock, crawl onto the pointy part of the rock, and then dive from there into the water. He would swim around then crawl back onto the rock and to the point and dive again. I watched him do this many times before I returned to my book.

The first winter I had Dennis, I became greatly concerned about him. He stopped eating. He didn't eat for three months. After the winter retreat, he began to eat again. I had a lot to learn about Dennis.

After Dennis finally outgrew the aquarium, I purchased another larger pool and placed it and Dennis in a habitat outside. Dennis lived in it for several years. He had a nice yard to walk around in.

Years later, I dug another pool in a different habitat. While it was still new, I tried Dennis in it. I watched as he walked to the very bottom of the pool. Over the years, Dennis had gained considerable weight. He no longer floated to the top of the pool. He had weight enough to sustain his balance. I knew then that Dennis would be okay in the pond if he should decide to go there. Dennis stayed a few days in the new pool and decided he would make his permanent home at the pond.

Not all special needs animals like Dennis have a happy ending but Dennis outgrew his handicap and was able to live the life that was meant to be for him. Instincts told him he should go to the pond. He had to answer the call of the wild.

Epilogue

My husband and I have tried to meet the needs of a growing population of abandoned, injured, rejected or unwanted animals since 1988. Every new animal presents a challenge. The animal must be taught to get along with the rest of the animals or be placed in a habitat where it can't be hurt or hurt the other animals. Puppies must be taught to not chase the ducks, leave the cats alone, quit harassing the older dogs, don't pull on the horse's tail, and don't chew on electrical cords.

We try to encourage birds not to build nests where the cats sit and wait for their baby birds to attempt their first flight. But occasionally, the cats will bring up a bird, or chipmunk, or a baby rabbit. If unharmed, we will hold these animals to be released in another location.

We allow nature to take its course in and around the pond. The wildlife is free to come and go at will. A variety of ducks have made pit stops, some staying for months. We always look forward to the Canadian Geese that stop on their yearly migration. They usually spend a few days resting before heading north again.

Caring for any animal can be time consuming. Feeding a baby bird may require intervals every hour from sunup to sundown. Old or sick animals may require medication throughout the day. A sick lamb may require bottle feeding. Dogs and cats need frequent trips to the veterinarian for spaying and neutering. Sutures need removal. The horses and sheep require worming. Some ailments may require hours of research to determine the cause. We adhere to State laws for inoculations and a rabies clinic is held each year for such purposes.

There are endless chores of feeding the animals, some with special diets. Foods are bought in bulk. Dog food, cat food, scratch feed, horse feed, goat feed and sheep feed are purchased weekly. The barns are filled with hay yearly, some square bales and some round bales whichever is available at the time.

Yet for all the time consuming chores of feeding, cleaning, and walking, there are rewards. A cat crawls into your lap and reaches to touch your face with her paw before she balls up in sleep in your lap. A puppy runs up to you while you have your hands in dirt planting a tree and puts his paw on your arm as if to say, "Can you give me just one little pat on the head?" A baby squirrel nurses the bottle in your hand and slowly closes its eyes in sleep content to remain in your hands. A baby woodpecker sticks its long tongue out to touch a little honey on the end of your finger.

What a grand Creator we have who has made all creation for His glory. I can only imagine how wonderful it must have been in the Garden of Eden (before the fall) when all the animals and mankind were at peace with one another. I praise God for sending animals throughout my existence for they have enriched my life and deepened my understanding of the Creator.

To The Reader

Working with animals can be a rewarding adventure; however, it can be time consuming. It requires discipline and a structured environment. Sometimes it is a thankless task. The only reward you may receive is a lick on the face from a happy dog.

Watching and studying the habitat of animals can enhance the wonderment of God's creation. Each species or subspecies can stupefy you with its complexity. Yet, God pronounced *good* once He created it. It is the hope of the author that you can come to a saving knowledge of the Lord Jesus Christ and enjoy His creation to the fullest.

Jesus Christ paid the price for all man's sins by His sacrificial death on the cross. Jesus is the *only* way to Heaven. You must realize you are a sinner in need of salvation. You can repent and ask Jesus into your heart with a simple prayer. If you confess Him, He will confess you. "If thou shalt confess with thy mouth the Lord Jesus and shalt believe in thine heart that God hath raised him from the dead, thou shalt be saved" Romans 10:9.

About The Author

Judean W. Etheredge, D. P. C., works part-time as a counselor with Autumn Olive Outreach. Prior to counseling, she worked as a social worker. She has loved and worked with animals all her life.

Previous works include: Cabin by the Lake, Cabin in the Pines, and Cabin by the Bridge.

Other interests include photography, art, and Bible collecting. She and her husband Richard live in rural south Alabama. You may contact her at Autumn Olive Ministries, 96 County Road 67, Thomasville, AL 36784.